The Graphic Novel

BEAUTY AND THE BEAST

RETOLD BY MICHAEL DAHL

ILLUSTRATED BY LUKE FELDMAN

Graphic Spin is published by Stone Arch Books
151 Good Counsel Drive, P.O. Box 669
Mankato, Minnesota 56002
www.stonearchbooks.com

Library of Congress Cataloging-in-Publication Data
Dahl, Michael.
    Beauty and the Beast: The Graphic Novel / retold by Michael Dahl; illustrated by Luke
Feldman.
    p. cm. — (Graphic Spin)
    ISBN 978-1-4342-0765-4 (library binding)
    ISBN 978-1-4342-0861-3 (pbk.)
    1. Graphic novels. [1. Graphic novels. 2. Fairy tales. 3. Folklore—France.] I. Feldman, Luke, ill.
II. Beauty and the beast. English. III. Title.
PZ7.7.D14Be 2009
[Fic]—dc22   2008006719

Summary: In a dark forest, a merchant picks a rose for his daughter Beauty. It belongs to a terrible
beast. To save his life, the merchant promises that his daughter will visit the creature. When she does,
Beauty grows to like the beast. But can she ever love him?

Art Director: Heather Kindseth
Graphic Designer: Kay Fraser

Librarian Reviewer
Katharine Kan
Graphic novel reviewer and Library Consultant, Panama City, FL
MLS in Library and Information Studies, University of Hawaii at Manoa, HI

Reading Consultant
Elizabeth Stedem
Educator/Consultant, Colorado Springs, CO
MA in Elementary Education, University of Denver, CO

1 2 3 4 5 6 13 12 11 10 09 08

Printed in the United States of America

CAST OF CHARACTERS

THE SISTERS

THE FATHER

BEAUTY

THE BEAST

Many years ago, in a faraway kingdom, in a town that sat by the sea . . .

A rich merchant lived at the top of a high hill with his three daughters.

The youngest daughter was the loveliest and the kindest of the three. So the merchant called her Beauty.

17

Because Beauty loved her father, she agreed to visit the monster the very next morning.

This is the place that Father described.

21

The Beast treated her with kindness and tenderness. He gave her presents every day. He treated her as a guest and not a prisoner.

Beauty told the creature that she wanted them to be good friends.

But at the end of every dinner, it was always the same.

Beauty, will you marry me?

I'm sorry, but I cannot marry you.

How could I marry a beast?

23

At the merchant's house . . .

. . . it was a happy reunion.

That night, Beauty told the family about her time with the beast.

Truth to tell, Beauty's sisters were a little jealous. They saw the fine clothes and precious jewels that the Beast had given her as presents.

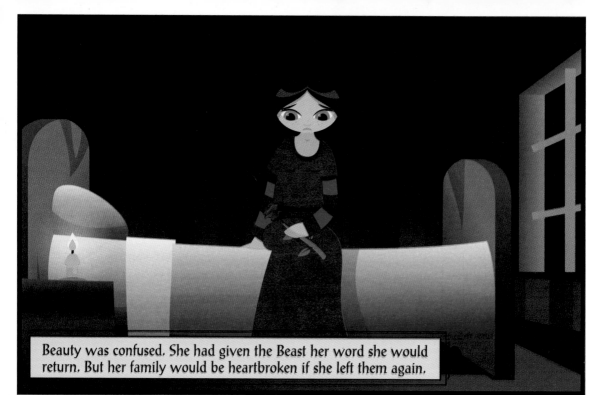

Beauty was confused. She had given the Beast her word she would return. But her family would be heartbroken if she left them again.

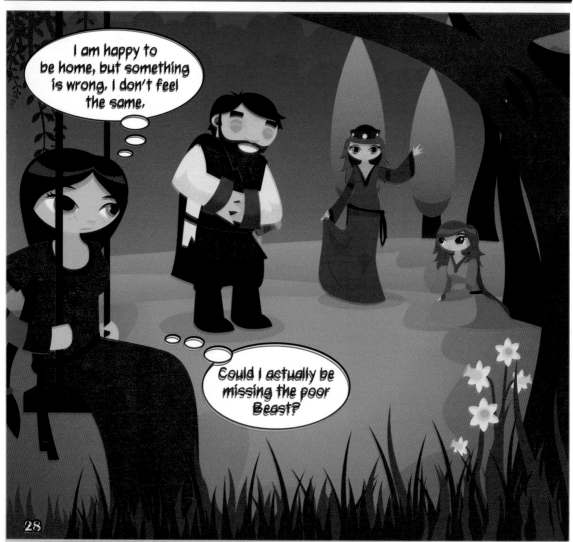

I am happy to be home, but something is wrong. I don't feel the same.

Could I actually be missing the poor Beast?

One night, Beauty slipped out of her room. She had made up her mind to keep her promise.

But when she finally reached the castle . . .

You said you would come back in a week. You promised.

Please forgive me. My family wanted me to stay.

It is too late now anyway. I am dying.

No! No! You cannot die, dear Beast. I love you!

No matter how my beast looks, I know he has a courageous and loyal heart.

And now that heart belongs to you.

And they lived happily together forever.

ABOUT THE AUTHOR

Michael Dahl is the author of more than 100 books for children and young adults. He has twice won the AEP Distinguished Achievement Award for his nonfiction. His Finnegan Zwake mystery series was chosen by the Agatha Awards to be among the five best mystery books for children in 2002 and 2003. He collects books on poison and graveyards, and lives in a haunted house in Minneapolis, Minnesota.

ABOUT THE ILLUSTRATOR

Luke Feldman is an illustrator, animator, and designer from Australia. For more than 10 years, he has worked on high-profile projects for large corporations such as Microsoft and Coca Cola. He has also worked closely with the Australian education department, developing animations and interactive games for children.

GLOSSARY

carriage (KA-rij)—a vehicle with wheels, often pulled by horses

courageous (kur-RAY-juhss)—brave or fearless

demands (di-MANDZ)—asks for something firmly

described (di-SKRIBED)—created a picture of something in words

expensive (ek-SPEN-siv)—costing a lot of money

kindness (KINDE-ness)—if someone shows kindness, he or she is being friendly, helpful, and generous

loyal (LOI-uhl)—firm in supporting or faithful to one's country, family, friends, or beliefs

maiden (MAYD-uhn)—a young, unmarried woman

merchant (MUR-chuhnt)—someone who sells goods for profit

precious (PRESH-uhss)—rare and valuable

reunion (ree-YOON-yuhn)—a meeting between people who have not seen each other for a long time

tenderness (TEN-dur-ness)—if someone shows tenderness, he or she is being gentle or kind

THE HISTORY OF BEAUTY AND THE BEAST

The tale of BEAUTY AND THE BEAST begins hundreds of years ago. Even before it was first written down, the story had been passed from person to person for many generations.

Partly inspired by these oral tales, French author Madame Gabrielle de Villeneuve wrote the first-known version of BEAUTY AND THE BEAST in 1740. Villeneuve meant for her story to be read by adults rather than children. The novella, or medium-length story, was nearly as long as a novel. It contained many parts that were later taken out, including information about the beast's childhood. Possibly the biggest difference, however, comes at the end of Villeneuve's tale. In her version, the beast is never transformed back into a prince. This part of the story was added 16 years later.

In 1756, another French author named Madame Le Prince de Beaumont crafted the best-known version of the fairy tale. Beaumont's tale was much shorter than Villeneuve's story. It was also aimed at younger readers. The new version quickly became popular, and a year later the story had been translated from French to English.

Since then, the story has been retold thousands of times in books, plays, and on film. On November 13, 1991, the Walt Disney Company released the animated version of BEAUTY AND THE BEAST to theaters. The film quickly became a success. It is the only animated picture to ever be nominated for the Academy Award for Best Picture.

DISCUSSION QUESTIONS

1. Beauty's father asks his daughters what they would like him to bring back from his trip. Two of the daughters want dresses and jewels, but Beauty wants just one rose. What does this tell you about Beauty's character? What kind of person is she?

2. Beauty's family didn't want her to return to the Beast's castle. Why do you think Beauty chose to return anyway?

3. Fairy tales are often told over and over again. Have you heard the Beauty and the Beast fairy tale before? How is this version of the story different from other versions you've heard, seen, or read?

WRITING PROMPTS

1. Fairy tales are fantasy stories, often about wizards, goblins, giants, and fairies. Many fairy tales have a happy ending. Write your own fairy tale. Then, read it to a friend or family member.

2. Beauty's father said that his daughters could have anything they wished for. If you could have anything, what would it be? Describe why you made that choice.

3. The story says that Beauty and the Beast "live happily together forever." Write a story about their life together. Will they get married? Will Beauty's family come to live with them? Use your imagination.

INTERNET SITES

The book may be over, but the adventure is just beginning.

Do you want to read more about the subjects or ideas in this book? Want to play cool games or watch videos about the authors who write these books? Then go to FactHound. At *www.facthound.com*, you'll be able to do all that, and more. The FactHound website can also send you to other safe Internet sites.

CHECK IT OUT!